Saint Polycarp, Blomfield Jackson

St. Polycarp, Bishop of Smyrna

Saint Polycarp, Blomfield Jackson

St. Polycarp, Bishop of Smyrna

ISBN/EAN: 9783743337527

Manufactured in Europe, USA, Canada, Australia, Japa

Cover: Foto ©Raphael Reischuk / pixelio.de

Manufactured and distributed by brebook publishing software
(www.brebook.com)

Saint Polycarp, Blomfield Jackson

St. Polycarp, Bishop of Smyrna

CONTENTS

PREFACE

THIS translation of the one extant Letter of St. Polycarp, and of the Letter of the Smyrnæans narrating his martyrdom, is designed to put within the reach of English readers in a handy form two of the most valuable of the classics of the Church. In point of time the Epistle of Polycarp is one of the writings which come very near to those of canonical authority. It may with reasonable probability be placed within some quarter of a century after the publication of St. John's Gospel, a somewhat shorter interval separating it from the Epistle of St. Clement. It appears to have been read in public at least as late as the time of Jerome, who in his *de Viris Illust.* xvii. calls it "valde utilem epistolam quæ usque hodie in Asiæ conventu legitur." It perhaps hardly deserves the depreciatory description of being "but a commonplace echo of the apostolic epistles" (D.C.B. iv. 424), but it is distinctly inferior in literary power to the Letters of Clement and Ignatius. One of the chief reasons why it is valuable is that it does "echo" canonical writings, and proves their dissemination and acceptance at the time of its composition. Unlike the Epistle of Clement, who was brought up amid Jewish associations, it shows far less familiarity with Hebrew Literature than with apostolic writings. Its reproduction of apostolic thought is obvious in cases where no verbal correspondence can be asserted. Special attention is called by marked type in this edition to instances of unquestionable quotation and reference, and these, if less numerous than those claimed for it in

some quarters, afford a remarkable vindication of Epistles
of St. Paul of which the genuineness has been assailed,
and are quite incompatible with any antagonism between
the supposed rival Johannine school and Pauline school.

The Letter of the Smyrnæans embodies the fullest and
not the least affecting contemporary narrative of an early
martyrdom.   The faith, constancy, and courtesy of the
aged Bishop are a striking illustration of the power work-
ing in the Roman world since Pentecost, and gradually
subduing it.   With the exception of the obvious interpolation or misreading of the "dove" in Chap. xvi. there
is nothing of the grotesquely marvellous which disfigures
some later stories.   The placing of the martyrdom under
Antoninus Pius furnishes an illustration of the fact that the
reigns of "good" emperors were not good times for the
Church.   The period between A.D. 98 and 180, covering
the generally beneficent reigns of Trajan, Hadrian,
Antoninus Pius, and Marcus Aurelius, includes famous
persecutions.   The accession of the brutal Commodus
brought relief.   So long as Christianity was not a " Religio
Licita " it was always open to a zealous or hostile magistrate to put unrepealed edicts in force.   Bishop Lightfoot
dates the martyrdom of Publius Bishop of Athens (Euseb.
Hist. Ecc. iv. 23), and of Ptolemæus and Lucius (Justin,
Apol. ii. 2), as well as that of Polycarp and his companions, in the reign of Antoninus Pius.   The second of
these cases supplies a striking illustration of the state of
things normally obtaining in the empire.   Arrest might
come at any moment, without organized and general
persecution.   The form of procedure indicates that later
reigns saw no abrogation of the principle formulated under
Trajan, that the bare confession of Christianity was held
to be a capital offence irrespectively of any moral offences
included in an accusation.

ST. POLYCARP

I

EARLY REFERENCES TO ST. POLYCARP AND
HIS MARTYRDOM, AND QUOTATIONS FROM
HIS EPISTLE

1. IGNATIUS, Bishop of Antioch, writing *c.*
A.D. 110:

(*a*) " I would give my life for you, and for
them whom for God's honour you sent to
Smyrna, from which place I am writing to you,
giving thanks to the Lord, loving Polycarp even
as I love you."—*Eph.* xxi.

(*β*) " The Ephesians from Smyrna, from which
place I am writing to you, salute you. They
are here with me for the glory of God, just as
you are (*i. e.* in the persons of their envoys), and
they have in all things refreshed me, together
with Polycarp, Bishop of the Smyrnæans."—
Mag. xv.

(γ) " I salute your holy Bishop and venerable presbytery and the deacons my fellow servants." —*Smyrn.* xii.

(δ) " Ignatius to Polycarp, Bishop of the Church of the Smyrnæans, . . . hearty greeting."—*Polyc. Inscr.* etc.

II. The " Shepherd " of Hermas, *c.* A.D. 150. The references here are less obvious and direct than in other authors, but Dr. C. Taylor (*Journal of Philology*, xx.) is of opinion that Hermas knew and used Polycarp's Epistle : *e. g.* Hermas, *Mand.* xii. i. 1, on "bridling" and "fighting lust," would appear to be in connection with both James i. 26 and iii. 2, and Polycarp, *Ep.* § 5. Again the remarkable description of " widows " as an " Altar of God," in connexion with the charge to " make supplication unceasingly," suggests parallels with Hermas, *Mand.* x. iii. 2; *Sim.* ii. 5, v. 3, 7, and ix. 27.

III. Letter of the Smyrnæans, *c.* A.D. 156, translated herein.

IV. Lucian, the witty *littérateur* of Samosata, writing *c.* A.D. 165-170. Bishop Lightfoot (*Apost. Fathers*, II. i. p. 606) enumerates the possible references to the martyrdom of Polycarp in the satire on the Death of Peregrinus, who committed suicide at the Olympic Games of A.D. 165. Salient points are (i) the lighting of the pyre with torches and fagots, (ii) the stripping off the clothes, (iii) the prayer on the pyre, (iv) the comparison with a baking, and (v) the eagerness of the crowd for relics.

V. Irenæus, Bishop of Lyons, † c. A.D. 200.

(a) *Adv. Hær.* iii. 3 ; cf. Euseb. *Hist. Ecc.* iv. 14. "Polycarp too, who was not only instructed by Apostles, and had been the companion of many that had seen the Christ, but had also been appointed for Asia by Apostles as Bishop of the Church in Smyrna. We ourselves have seen him in our early manhood, for he long survived and departed this life at a great age, after a glorious and most splendid martyrdom. He constantly taught what he had learned from the Apostles, what the Church hands down, and what alone is true."

In the continuation of this passage, Irenæus refers to the visit of Polycarp to Rome to confer with Anicetus, who was Bishop of Rome c. A.D. 153-155. "There are those," he adds, "who have heard him tell how John, the disciple of the Lord, when he went to take a bath in Ephesus, and saw Cerinthus within, rushed away from the bath without bathing, with the words, 'Let us flee, lest the room should even fall in, for Cerinthus, the enemy of the truth, is within.' Yea, and Polycarp himself also, when Marcion on one occasion confronted him, and said 'Recognise us,' replied, 'Aye, aye, I recognise the first-born of Satan.' So great care did the Apostles and their disciples take not to hold any communication, even by word, with any of those who falsify the truth, as Paul also said, 'A man that is an heretic, after the first and second admonition reject ; knowing that he that is such is subverted and sinneth, being condemned of himself.' "

(β) In the Letter to Victor (Euseb. *H.E.* v. 24): " When the blessed Polycarp sojourned at Rome in the days of Anicetus, they had some slight difference with one another, on this and on other matters. They did not care to have any strife on this point, and at once made peace. On the one hand Anicetus was unable to persuade Polycarp not to observe the customs which he had always observed with John, the Lord's disciple, and with the rest of the Apostles in whose company he had lived. Nor on the other hand did Polycarp persuade Anicetus to observe them, for he urged that he ought to hold to the practice of the presbyters before him. Under these circumstances they communicated together, and in the Church Anicetus yielded the Eucharist [1] to Polycarp, plainly as a mark of respect ; thus

[1] *i. e.* the privilege of offering the eucharistic sacrifice.

both parties, the observer and the non-observers, kept the peace of the whole Church, and so parted."

(γ) In the *Adv. Hær.* v. 33, § 4, Irenæus speaks of Papias (Bishop of Hierapolis, † *c.* A.D. 140), "hearer of John and a companion of Polycarp."

(δ) In his Letter to Florinus (Euseb. *Hist. Ecc.* v. 20) Irenæus writes—"When I was still a boy, I saw thee in Lower Asia at Polycarp's, faring splendidly in the imperial court, and endeavouring to stand well with him. For I remember the events of that time more clearly than what is of recent occurrence. The lessons learned in childhood grow with the growth of the soul, and become one with it ; and so I am able to tell even the spot where the blessed Polycarp used to sit and discourse, his goings out and his comings in, his manner of life, his personal appearance, and the public discourses which he used to give. I remember how he used to tell of his intercourse with John, and with the rest of those who had seen the Lord, and how he recalled and related their words. And such particulars as he had heard concerning the Lord, and concerning His mighty works, and concerning His teaching, Polycarp, as having derived them from the eye-witnesses of the life of the Word, used to tell without exception in harmony with the Scriptures. To these things by God s mercy I used to listen with all my might, noting them down from time to time, if not on paper, in my heart; and ever by God's grace I faithfully turn them over and over in my mind. And I am able to bear witness before God that if anything of the kind (*i. e.* the heresy previously referred to) had been heard by that blessed and apostolic elder he would have cried out, and stopped his ears, and with his familiar words, 'Oh good God, to what times hast Thou kept me that I should endure these things,' would have fled from the spot where he was sitting or standing when he had heard such words. And this can be made quite plain from the letters which he wrote whether to the Churches in his neighbourhood confirming them, or to certain of the brethren warning and exhorting them."

(ε) In the *Adv. Hær.* iii. 3, 4, Irenæus writes— " There is a very sufficient epistle of Polycarp written to the Philippians in which all who wish to do so, and care for their salvation, can learn both the character of his faith and of his preaching of the truth."

VI. Polycrates, Bishop of Ephesus, † *c.* A.D. 195.—Ep. ad Victorem ep. Rom. apud Euseb. *Hist. Ecc.* v. 24.

Enumerating the " great lights of Asia, who

have fallen asleep and shall rise again at the day of the Lord's coming," Polycrates mentions "Polycarp, bishop and martyr at Smyrna."

VII. Tertullian, writing, *c.* A.D. 200, † *c.* A.D. 240 : " Thus it is that Apostolic Churches hand down their registers ; as that of the Smyrnæans recalls Polycarp appointed by John." *De Præscr. Hæret.* xxxii.

VIII. " Acts of Pionius," a martyr at Smyrna, in the Decian persecution, March 12, A.D. 250 ; the date being fixed by the names of the consuls. Of the " Acts " two Latin forms of translation are extant (Bollandists, Feb. 1, and Ruinart, *Acta Sincera,* pp. 188, *et seq.*). " So on the second day of the sixth month, which is the IVth before the Ides of March, being a great Sabbath,[1] on the birthday of Polycarp the martyr, persecution overtook Pionius," etc.

[1] March 12 was not a Saturday in A.D. 250. Bishop Lightfoot considers the reference to the Sabbath an interpolation, and would " with some confidence " restore the chronological notice at the close of the Acts of Pionius as follows : " These things happened when Julius Proculus Quintilianus was Proconsul [of Asia], in the Consulship of [Imperator] Gaius Messius Quintus Trajanus Decius [Augustus] for the second time, and Vettius Gratus, according to Roman reckoning on the fourth before the Ides of March, according to Asiatic reckoning on the nineteenth day of the sixth month, at the tenth hour, but, according to the reckoning of us (Christians), etc.,

IX. Eusebius, Bishop of Cæsarea, † c. A.D. 340. In his *Chronicon*, Eusebius writes on the first year of Trajan (A.D. 98): "Irenæus states that the Apostle John lived till the time of Trajan. After him Papias of Hierapolis and Polycarp, Bishop of the Province of the Smyrnæans, were recognised as his disciples." And after the seventh year of M. Aurelius (A.D. 167): "Persecution attacking the Church, Polycarp underwent martyrdom. His martyrdom is committed to writing."[1]

In his *Ecc. Hist.* iii. 36, 38; iv. 14, 15, and v. 5 and 20, there are references to the life and martyrdom of Polycarp. (Cf. pp. 9, 10, 11.)

X. In the *Apostolical Constitutions*, of uncertain date, but in parts probably of the fourth century, there are three probable references to the Epistle of Polycarp, chap. iv.: "Our widows must be sober-minded . . . knowing that they are God's altar"; viz. in iii. 6; iii. 14, and iii. 26.

in the reign of our Lord Jesus Christ, etc."—Lightfoot *Apost. Fathers*, II. i. p. 721.

[1] This statement has been the main source of opinion as to the date of the martyrdom. But it is to be observed that it is placed not over against, but *after*, the date. And there immediately follows a reference to the persecutions at Vienne and Lyons in A.D. 177. Eusebius does not apparently mean to be more definite than that these martyrdoms happened about this period. See p. 73, *n.*

XI. Also of the latter part of the fourth century is probably the groundwork, if not the whole, of the fictitious *Life of Polycarp*, by Pionius, which incorporates the Epistle. It was published by the Bollandists in Latin, and a Greek Text was edited from a MS. in the Paris Library by Duchesne in 1881.

XII. To these may be added : St. Jerome, *c.* A.D. 400, *De Viris Illust.* xvii.; Socrates, *c.* A.D. 440, *Hist. Ecc.* v. 22 ; Sozomen, *c.* A.D. 455, *Hist. Ecc.* vii. 19 ; Theodoret, A.D. 446, *Ep.* cxlv. ; and, somewhat later, Antiochus of St. Saba, *c.* A.D. 610, as pointed out by Dr. Cotterill. (Cf. p. 18.)

The evidence of quotation and reference is therefore strong ; far stronger than can be adduced for the genuineness of some of the most generally accepted classics. "To the concurrent testimony of antiquity," says Bishop Lightfoot (*Apost. Fathers*, II. i. p. 582), "there is no dissentient voice."

II

INTERNAL EVIDENCE OF THE GENUINENESS OF THE EPISTLE TO THE PHILIPPIANS

I. THE style and composition are such as might be expected from a writer of deep personal piety and of familiarity with the Scriptures of the Church.

II. The position of influence implied is exactly what might be expected in the case of a favourite pupil of St. John.

III. There is no trace of anachronism ; of tone of thought or allusion proper to, or specially characteristic of, a later date.[1]

[1] An attempt has been made to show that the condemnation of heresy in § vii. refers to the Docetism of Marcion, who did not become notorious till the reign of Antoninus Pius, and was probably a small boy at the date of the Epistle. But it has been replied (cf. Bishop Lightfoot, *Apost. Fathers*, II. i. p. 585) that the assumption that Marcion is aimed at is as improbable as it is gratuitous : "not only is there nothing specially characteristic of Marcion in the heresy or heresies denounced by Polycarp, but some of the charges are quite inapplicable to him."

IV. Opponents of the genuineness of the Ignatian letters, with the questions touching which the defence of the Epistle of Polycarp is closely connected, have attributed both the Ignatian Letters and the Letter of Polycarp to one and the same imaginary forger.

The refutation of any such theory of common authorship lies in the fact of the obvious points of contrast marking the two works, a contrast, as Bishop Lightfoot remarks [*l. c.* p. 594], " more striking indeed than we should have expected to find between two Christian writers who lived at the same time, and were personally acquainted with each other." Among these points are :

(*a*) Scripture. The one short Letter of Polycarp contains much more quotation of the New Testament than the seven Letters of Ignatius, and where Ignatius does show familiarity with the New Testament it is mainly by allusion and turn of phrase. On the other hand, some students would go so far (*e. g.* Funk, *Die Echtheit der Ignatianischen Briefe,* p. 34, quoted by Lightfoot) as to reckon thirty-five direct quotations from the New Testament in Polycarp, twenty-two being from Apostolic Epistles.

(*β*) Doctrine. St. Polycarp is rather hortatory than didactic. In St. Ignatius we have plain statements as to the Incarnation, the real man-

B

hood, and the two natures of the Lord, and the Sacrament of the Eucharist, as in *Eph.* vi. xiii. xx. ; *Magn.* vii. ; *Trall.* viii. ; *Philad.* iv. etc. Nothing of the kind occurs in Polycarp.

(γ) The Church and Church Organisation. St. Ignatius is strong on the unity of the Church and the Episcopate. St. Polycarp is silent as to unity, and only implies the Episcopate in his salutation, " Polycarp and the Presbyters with him."

V. In the *Journal of Philology*, vol. xix. pp. 241-285, Dr. Cotterill argued that Antiochus, monk of Santa Saba, early in the seventh century, whose Homilies (Migne, *Greek Fathers*, lxxxix.) contain portions of the Epistle, was probably himself the author of the Epistle of Polycarp.

This novel theory has been elaborately refuted by Dr. C. Taylor, Master of St. John's College, Cambridge, in the *Journal of Philology*, vol. xx.

III

INTERNAL EVIDENCE OF THE GENUINENESS OF THE LETTER OF THE SMYRNÆANS ON THE MARTYRDOM OF ST. POLYCARP

THE narrative professes to be that of contemporaries and eye-witnesses. Do the contents of the document afford indications that it was the composition of a later date, more or less fabulous and legendary? The grounds on which some critics[1] have given an affirmative answer to this challenge are:

I. The miraculous element. Look, it has been said, at the dove (§ xvi.) issuing from the wound in the side, and at the flames (§ xv.) refusing to consume. What of the fragrance floating from the pyre? On these points see notes to the sections referred to.

II. Apparent anachronisms, e.g. the reverence paid to martyrs and their relics. On this too see

---

[1] e.g. Keim, who would place its date as late as A.D. 260-282 (*Aus dem Urchristenthum*, p. 130).

note on § xvii., and observe with Bishop Lightfoot, how only "half a century later Tertullian
uses language which shows that the ceremonial
commemoration of the dead was far more
developed than as here represented."—*De Coron.*
iii.

III. The use of the phrase "Catholic Church,"
supposed to indicate a later date than A.D. 155.
Why? Even if the word be genuine in § xvi.
where Polycarp is described in the Common
Text as "Bishop of the Catholic Church in
Smyrna," and the distinctive title be used to
distinguish the Catholic Church from heretical
sects, why not? There were already heretical
sects, and there are almost contemporary instances of the use of the word Catholic in this
sense (*e.g.* Clement of Alexandria, *Strom.* vii. 17).

IV. A subtler objection has been the apparently artificial character of the incidents recorded
as parallel to those of the Passion of our Lord.
Attention is specially called to the prediction of
death three days after apprehension (§ v.), to the
name of the officer "Herodes" (§ vi.), to the
treachery of one of the household (§ vi.), to the
apprehension near the city (§§ v., vi.), at night
(§ vii.), as a robber (§ vii.), to the words of
resignation, "God's will be done" (§ vii.), and to
the piercing of the body (§ xvi.).

But these are all natural and likely circumstances, and the tendency to group and represent them as reminders of the Passion of our Lord was so inevitable in the case of early martyrdoms as to call for no special remark. Obviously a fable-monger free to invent might have invented better coincidences than these. "The most striking coincidence," says Bishop Lightfoot, "is the name Herodes ; but this name was sufficiently frequent in Polycarp's time, and there is only a faint resemblance between the position of the Smyrnæan captain of police, who takes Polycarp into custody, and the Galilean King, whose part in the Passion was confined to insolent mockery, and who pronounced Jesus innocent of the charges brought against him. Here again a fabricator would have secured a better parallel. We may say generally that *the violence of the parallelism is a guarantee of the accuracy of the facts.*"—Bishop Lightfoot, *Apost. Fathers*, II. i. 613, 614.

IV

LIFE OF ST. POLYCARP

EXTANT genuine authorities for the life of Poly-carpus,[1] or Polycarp, of Smyrna, are confined to the passages already cited, and to materials to be gathered from the Letter of Polycarp and the Letter of the Smyrnæans.

The Pionian "Life," referred to on p. 15, is plainly unauthentic. It deals largely with a fantastic supernaturalism, quotes non-existent documents, and cannot be relied on. It may, however, preserve some true traditions. It relates how Polycarp was a little slave-boy, bought and brought up by a pious and wealthy widow named Callisto, who eventually made him her steward. He was ordained Deacon by Bucolos (a personage of possible historical character, and perhaps appointed Bishop of Smyrna by St. John), Bishop of Smyrna, who loved him as a

[1] The name Polycarpus, Πολύκαρπος, = fruitful, pro-ductive. Cf. Hom. *Od.* vii. 122, xxiv. 221. It was a common slave's name ; a Graffito at Pompeii advertises ' Polycarpus fugit.'

son. That he wrote " many " treatises, sermons
and letters, all destroyed by his persecutors
about the time of the martyrdom, is improbable,
for his extant Epistle gives no indications of
practice in literary composition. But it may
well have been one among several.[1]

The representation that he was a man of
property is corroborated by the mention of the
slave lads in the Letter of the Smyrnæans (§ vi.),
and by the probability that the homestead where
he was arrested, and where he offered hospitality
to the imperial officers, was his own (§§ vi., vii.).

Was Polycarp a married man? This has
been both asserted and denied on equally in-
sufficient evidence. Ignatius in his Letter to
Polycarp (§ v.) has been supposed to urge any
one professing virginity to beware of arrogance,
lest by acquiring greater fame than the Bishop he
be *ipso facto* defiled ; and so to imply that the
Bishop was not a celibate. But the true rendering of the passage is almost certainly not " if *he*
become known beyond the Bishop " but " if *it*
become known," *i.e.* if the profession of virginity
go beyond the ears of the Bishop. Again, the
fact that *Alce* is saluted in the Letter of Ignatius
to Polycarp (§ viii.) and in that to the Smyrnæans
(§ xiii.) is manifestly a slender support for the
conjecture that she was Polycarp's wife. But as

[1] Cf. Euseb. *Hist. Ecc.* v. 20, quoted on p. 12.

the marriage of the clergy was not yet seriously objected to in the second century either in East or West, there is no reason why Polycarp may not have lived in wedlock.

Of friendship with other Saints there is little to be said. His most famous contemporaries were Clement of Rome, Ignatius of Antioch, and Papias of the Phrygian Hierapolis. The first died long before Polycarp's visit to Rome, and it is not likely that these two great fathers ever met, but Po.ycarp shows himself familiar with Clement's Epistle to the Corinthians.

The statement of Irenæus (*Adv. Hær.* v. 33, § 4) that Papias was a "scholar of John and a companion of Polycarp" may be only an inference of the writer, but whatever may have been the earlier associations, it is unlikely that Polycarp and Papias, living only some hundred-and-fifty miles apart, should not have been in communication.

St. Polycarp is commemorated on January 26 in the Roman, Spanish, and German Calendars, probably from a confusion in Western Calendars between the great saint and two others of the same name. His name does not appear in the Sarum, Scottish, and old English lists. In the menology of Basil and in the Byzantine Calendar, as in the ancient Syriac martyrology of *c.* A.D. 350, it marks Feb. 23.[1]

[1] Cf. note on the Letter of the Smyrnæans, xxi. p. 73.

V

MSS. AND VERSIONS

(i) Of the Epistle of Polycarp.

a. MSS. The main authorities are :

1. Vaticanus (V.), eleventh century, containing among various patristic tracts and sermons the Ignatian Letters as well as the Epistle of Polycarp.
2. Ottobonianus (O.), in the Vatican Library, sixteenth century.
3. Florentinus (F.), in the Laurentian Library at Florence, sixteenth century.
4. Parisiensis (P.), sixteenth century.

all derived from V.

5. Casanatensis (C.), in the Library of the Minerva at Rome, qy. fifteenth century, containing Epistles of Polycarp and Barnabas.
6. Barberinus (B.), in the Barberini Library at Rome, sixteenth century.
7. Neapolitanus (N.), a paper MS. of the fifteenth century, in the National Library at Naples.

b. VERSIONS. The oldest MS. of the Latin Version is not older than the ninth century. The translation into Latin is loose and indicative of corruption in the original.

There is no known Syriac version.

(ii) Of the Letter of the Smyrnæans.

a. MSS.

1. Mosquensis (M.), thirteenth century, in the Library of the Holy Synod at Moscow.   Greek.
2. Baroccianus, of the eleventh century, imperfect : in the Bodleian.   Greek.
3. Paris, tenth century.   Greek.
4. Vindobonensis, twelfth century, at Vienna. Greek.
5. Jerusalem, tenth century.   Greek.

b. Versions.

Latin, various.   See Harnack, *Die Zeit des Ignatius*, pp. 77, *et seq.*, and Lightfoot, *Apost. Fathers*, II. iii. p. 358.

There is a Syriac version in the British Museum, and a Coptic in the Vatican, both being derived from Eusebius, and not from the actual Letter.

VI

SUGGESTED CHRONOLOGICAL TABLE

A.D.	Emperors of Rome.	Events.	Polycarp.
55	Nero Imp.	—	—
59	—	—	? Birth.
68	Galba Imp.	Martyrdom of St. Paul.	
69	Otho, Vitellius Vespasian, Imp.	— —	? Birth. Baptism.
70	—	Capture of Jerusalem.	— —
79	Titus Imp.	—	—
81	Domitian Imp.	—	—
96	Nerva Imp.	—	—
98	Trajan Imp.	? Ep. of St. Clement.	—.
c. 99	—	Death of St. Clement.	Bishop of Smyrna.
c. 100	—	Death of St. John.	—
c. 110	—	Martyrdom of St. Ignatius.	Ep. to Philippians.
117	Hadrian Imp.	—	—
138	Antoninus Pius Imp.	—	—
c. 150	—	Hermas writes the " Shepherd."	—
155	—	—	Visit to Rome.
155	—	—	Martyrdom, Feb. 23.
156	—	—	Letter of Smyrnæans.

VII

THE EPISTLE OF POLYCARP TO THE PHILIPPIANS

POLYCARP and the Presbyters that are with him [1] to the Church of God that is sojourning [2] at Philippi, mercy to you and peace from Almighty God and Jesus Christ our Saviour " **be multiplied** " (1 Pet. i. 2 ; 2 Pet. i. 2 ; Jude 2).

[1] The Bishop associates himself with his presbyters. St. Paul, writing to the same Church some forty-eight years earlier, salutes the Saints, "with the bishops and deacons," "Episcopus" in A.D. 62 being a title used of presbyters ; by A.D. 110 it is confined to the "distinguished men" (Clem. *Cor.* xliv.) who have succeeded the Apostles in the special functions of ordaining, confirming, and ruling. So Bishop Lightfoot, "Polycarp evidently writes here as a bishop in the later and fuller sense of the title, surrounded by his Council of presbyters."

[2] *Sojourning.* The Greek word is first so used by St. Clement (*Cor.*), and became general. The correlative substantive *paroikia* originally meant place of sojourning for the local Church and bishop, and so was equivalent to our *diocese*. Hence through the Latin *parochia* and the French *paroisse* it passed into our *parish*. The familiar word will remind dwellers in the "parish" that, like Abraham (Heb. xi. 9), they "*sojourn* in a land of promise." Cf. note on p. 48.

I. I rejoiced greatly with you in our Lord Jesus Christ on your receiving the copies [1] of the true Love, and escorting on their way, as it fell to your lot to do,[2] the men enwrapped in their chains,[3] seemly ornament of Saints, in that they are diadems of them that are truly chosen by God and by our Lord ; [4] and because the firm root of your faith, proclaimed from times of old,[5] abides unto this present time, and "**brings forth fruit**" (Col. i. 6) unto our Lord Jesus Christ,

[1] Counterfeits, in a good sense : the word *mimema* is a correlative of that rendered "followers" or "imitators" in R. V. 1 Cor. iv. 16; Eph. v. 1; 1 Thess. i. 6, ii. 14 ; Heb. vi. 12, and 1 Pet. iii. 13.

[2] Bishop Lightfoot translates "as befitted you," but this is not quite the force of the word rightly rendered in his notes "it pertaineth to you"; it is the word describing the portion of goods that "*fell*" to the prodigal (Luke xv. 12).

[3] Probably Ignatius, Zosimus, and Rufus (cf. cap. ix.).

[4] The red dragon of the Apocalypse had seven "diadems" upon his heads (Rev. xii. 3), and so the beast out of the sea (Rev. xiii. 1). The Rider on the white horse (Rev. xix. 12) had on his head many "diadems." The word occurs nowhere else in the New Testament. In Clem. *Hom.* xii. 20, Truth is the "diadem" of the everlasting Kingdom. Cf. Hermas, *Mand.* xii. 25, for the "crowning." "Nothing in this exordium is commonplace" (Taylor).

[5] *i. e.* from the earliest days of the spread of the Gospel. —Cf. Phil. iv. 15, and chap. vii. p. 39. "This excellent summary of faith," *i. e.* Acts xvi. 31, "we find also but with a very little paraphrase propounded as sufficient by St.

Who endured to come so far as to death for our sins, Whom God raised, "**having loosed the pains of death**" (Acts ii. 24), in "**whom, not having seen, ye**" trust "**with joy unspeakable and full of glory**" (1 Pet. i. 8). Into this joy many long to enter, knowing that [1] "**by grace ye are saved**," "**not of works**" (Eph. ii. 5, 8, 9), but by God's will through Jesus Christ.

II. Therefore "**Gird up**" your "**loins**" (1 Pet. i. 13) and "**serve**" God "**in fear**" (Ps. ii. 11) and truth; leave the vain talking [2] and the error of the many; "**trust in God Who raised**" our Lord Jesus Christ "**from the dead, and gave Him glory**" (1 Pet. i. 21) and a Throne on His right hand; to Whom were subjected all things in heaven and on earth [3]; Whom "**everything that hath breath**" [4] (Ps. cl. 6) serves; Who is coming as "**Judge of quick and dead**" (Acts x. 42); Whose blood God will require of them that disobey Him. But He that raised Him from the dead

---

Polycarp in that excellent epistle of his to the Philippians."—Jer. Taylor, *Duct. Dub.* ii. 3, § 67.

[1] Bishop Lightfoot points out that by this phrase Polycarp seems to introduce quotations. Cf. chapters iv. v. vi.

[2] The original is rendered in 1 Tim. i. 6 in A. V. "vain jangling," and in R. V. as above.

[3] Cf. 1 Cor. xv. 28; Phil. ii. 10, and iii. 21.

[4] Cf. 1 Kings xv. 29, LXX.

will raise us also,[1] if we do His will and walk
in His commandments, and love what He
loved, holding off from all unrighteousness,
covetousness, love of money,[2] backbiting, false
witness, "**not rendering evil for evil or railing for
railing**" (1 Pet. iii. 9), or cuff[3] for cuff, or curse
for curse, remembering what the Lord said,
teaching "**Judge not, that ye be not judged**"
(Matt. vii. 1); forgive and it shall be forgiven
unto you; be ye merciful, that ye be shewn
mercy;[4] "**With what measure ye mete it shall be
measured to you again**" (Matt. vii. 2); and
"**Blessed are the poor**" (Matt. v. 3) and they that
are being "**persecuted for righteousness sake,
for theirs is the kingdom** of God"[5] (Matt. v. 10).

III. Not, brethren, in concession to my own

[1] Cf. 2 Cor. iv. 14.

[2] The original occurs in the New Testament only in
1 Tim. vi. 10.

[3] The original ($\gamma\rho\acute{o}\nu\theta os$) is a late word for *fist*, and so a
blow with the fist.

[4] These charges do not verbally tally with the canonical gospels, but convey the sense of Matt. vi. 14, and Luke
vi. 36, though the word rendered "merciful" is not the
same as Polycarp's. They may preserve sayings not
recorded in Scripture.

[5] In Matt. v. 10 our Lord uses the perfect tense, Blessed
are they which *have been* persecuted, as in Revised Version. The blessing comes after the faithful endurance of
persecution. Polycarp's present tense conveys his thought

inclination, but because you challenged me,[1] am I writing to you concerning righteousness. For neither have I nor has any other like me ability to follow hard on the wisdom[2] of the blessed and glorious Paul, who, when he had come among you, in the presence of them of that time,[3] taught accurately and constantly the word of truth[4] and, when absent,[5] wrote to you letters,[6] into which if you examine carefully you will be enabled to be

---

of a blessing even in persecution. Observe the omission of "in spirit" after "poor," and the substitution of " God " for "heaven" as in Luke vi. 20. " In selecting these two beatitudes Polycarp is guided by the fact that to these two alone the promise of the kingdom of heaven is attached " (Bishop Lightfoot).

[1] Polycarp would have been too modest to exhort the Philippians had they not asked for his exhortation. The reading προεπεκαλέσασθε, challenged, is supported by the Latin *provocastis*, and is unobjectionable Greek. There is MS. authority for προεπηλακίσασθε, literally, bespattered with mud, or reproached, a dubious grammatical form.

[2] The Philippians have a pre-eminent counsellor in St. Paul. Cf. 2 Pet. iii. 15.

[3] *i.e.* A.D. 52.

[4] Lit. the word concerning truth ; *i.e.* the true doctrine.

[5] Cf. 2 Cor. x. 1.

[6] The plural *may* indicate an impression on Polycarp's part that the Philippians were in possession of more than one letter from St. Paul addressed to their Church. But the use of the plural to designate a single letter is not infrequent, *e.g.* Eurip. I. A. 111.

built up into the faith given to you, "**which is the Mother of us all**"[1] (Gal. iv. 26), with hope following after, and love towards God and Christ and our neighbour going before.[2] For if any one be surrounded by, and occupied in,[3] these, he hath fulfilled (Rom. xiii. 8 and Gal. v. 14) the commandment of righteousness. For he that hath love is far from all sin.[4]

IV. Now love of money is the beginning of all difficulties.[5] Knowing[6] then that "**we brought nothing into the world**" and "**neither can we carry anything out**" (1 Tim. vi. 7), let us arm ourselves with "**the arms of righteousness**"[7] (2 Cor. vi. 7), and teach ourselves first to walk in the

---

[1] The coincidence may be merely verbal and fortuitous. Jacobson, Lightfoot and others quote *The Martyrdom of Justin*, § iv., "Our true Father is the Christ, and our mother our faith in Him." Cf. Hermas, *Vis.* viii. 2-6, where Faith is mother and ancestress of Virtues.

[2] *i. e.* before Hope. After Faith comes Hope preceded by Charity. Faith begets Charity or Love, and Hope follows. Cf. 1 Thess. i. 3 and Col. i. 4, 5. In 1 Cor. xiii. 13 Charity comes last as being the permanent survivor of the Great Three.

[3] Lit. "be *within* these." Bishop Lightfoot compares Plutarch, *Vit. Hom.* 6, "within," *i. e.* "occupied in every science and art." Cf. Horace's "totus in illis," *Sat.* i. ix. 1.

[4] Cf. Rom. xiii. 10.   [5] Cf. 1 Tim. vi. 10.

[6] Cf. p. 30, note.

[7] Cf. Rom. vi. 13, where our members are to be "instruments" or "weapons" (R. V. marg.) of righteousness.

commandment of the Lord ; next also your
wives, in the faith given unto them, and in love
and in chastity, cherishing [1] their own husbands
in all truth,[2] and loving all men alike in all con-
tinency, to train up their children too in the
training of the fear of the Lord. [Let us teach]
the widows too to be temperate [3] concerning the
faith of the Lord, making supplication unceasingly for all, being far removed from all calumny,
backbiting, false witness, love of money, and
every evil ; knowing that they are God's Altar,[4]

[1] The original word does not occur in the New
Testament, but is frequent in classical Greek for family
affection. Cf. Clem. *Cor.* i.

[2] *i. e.* with true, faithful affection.

[3] "Their religion must not be a frenzy of fanaticism,
but a calm confidence" (Lightfoot). Cf. 1 Tim. iii. 11
and v. 5.

[4] The word in the original, thysiasterion (= place of
sacrifice, whether bloody or unbloody), is the regular
LXX. and New Testament term for the altar used in
the worship of Jehovah. Its more extended use in the
literature of the Church begins with the famous passage
in Heb. xiii. 10, "we have an altar." Bishop Lightfoot
compares Tertullian *ad Ux.* i. 7 : "Cum viduam adlegi
in ordinem, nisi univiram, non concedat ; aram enim
Dei mundam proponi oportet." For figurative uses of
the word in the Ignatian letters, see *Eph.* 5, *Mag.* 7,
Trall. 7, *Rom.* 2, and *Philad.* 4. "They themselves are
the altar ; their thoughts, words, and deeds, more especially their prayers, are the sacrifices offered" (Lightfoot).
Cf. also Introduction, pp. 8, 14.

and that all things are examined to see if there be blemish in them, and that there is hid from Him nor thought nor intention nor any of "**the secrets of our heart**" (1 Cor. xiv. 25).

V. Knowing[1] then that "**God is not mocked**" (Gal. vi. 7), we ought to walk worthily of His commandment and glory.[2] In like manner should the deacons be blameless before His righteousness, as deacons of God and Christ, and not of men; not slanderers, not double-tongued,[3] not lovers of money, continent in all things, tender-hearted,[4] careful, walking according to the truth of the Lord, Who was made "deacon"[5] of all. To Him if we be well pleasing in this present world we shall also receive as our reward the world to come, in accordance with His promise to us to raise us from the dead, and because, if our conversation[6] be worthy of Him, "**we shall also reign with Him**"[7]

[1] Cf. note on p. 30.

[2] Cf. 1 Thess. ii. 12, and Herm. *Vis.* i. and iii.

[3] Bishop Lightfoot prefers "tale-bearers." Cf. 1 Tim. iii. 1—13.

[4] Cf. Eph. iv. 32, and Hermas, *Sim.* ix. 24, 2.

[5] The paronomasia is lost in the rendering "minister" or "servant." Cf. Matt. xx. 28, and Mark ix. 35.

[6] Phil. i. 27 ; cf. Clem. *Cor.* 21.

[7] St. Paul here seems to have quoted some primitive hymn or formula. Cf. Alford *in loc.* 1 Tim. iii. 16 may be another such citation.

(2 Tim. ii. 12), if indeed we believe. In like manner let the younger men be blameless in all things, above everything taking heed for purity, bridling[1] themselves from every evil. For it is good to be checked from following[2] the lusts in the world, for every lust warreth against the Spirit,[3] and "**neither fornicators nor effeminate, nor abusers of themselves with mankind shall inherit the kingdom of God**" (1 Cor. vi. 9, 10), nor they that do iniquity. Wherefore they are bound to abstain from all these things, being subject to the presbyters and deacons[4] as to God and Christ. And the virgins must walk in a blameless and pure conscience.

VI. And that the presbyters be tender-

---

[1] Cf. Jas. i. 26, iii. 2.

[2] Cf. Gal. v. 7 ; the word rendered "hinder."

[3] Cf. 1 John ii. 15, 16 ; 1 Pet. ii. 11, and Gal. v. 17.

[4] Bishop Lightfoot contrasts Ign. *Mag.* vi. where the supreme authority is vested in the Bishop. "Either, therefore, there was no Bishop at Philippi when Polycarp wrote, or Polycarp did not think fit to separate his claims to allegiance from this of the presbyters." Yet if the moral conduct of the younger men came naturally more immediately under the supervision of the presbyters Polycarp might as naturally recommend obedience to them ; omission of mention of the Bishop would tell as little for or against the presence of a Bishop at Philippi as a similar admonition to the young men of London would prove or disprove the existence of a Bishop of London.

hearted,[1] compassionate to all, turning home-ward the strayed sheep, visiting all that are sick, not neglecting widow or orphan or poor man, but providing ever what is good before God and man,[2] abstaining from all wrath, respect of persons, unjust judgment, being far removed from all love of money, not quickly believing anything against any one, not hasty in judg-ment, knowing that we are all debtors of sin.[3] If then we ask of the Lord to forgive us, we ought also to forgive.[4] For we are before the eyes of the Lord and God, and we must "**all stand before the judgment seat of Christ**"[5] (Rom. xiv. 10), and give each an account for himself.[6] Thus then let us serve Him with fear and reverence [7] as He Himself charged us, and the Apostles who evangelized us [8] and the prophets who preached beforehand the coming of our Lord, zealous

[1] Cf. note on § v. [2] Cf. 2 Cor. viii. 21.
[3] "The meaning seems to be, we have contracted obligations of sin. Cf. Rom. iii. 9" (Lightfoot). The phrase "knowing that" may indicate a quotation. Cf. note on p. 30. [4] Cf. Matt. vi. 12, 14, 15.
[5] R. V. follows the reading "**of God**" with the over-whelming support of A, B, C¹, D, E, F, G. Polycarp may rather have in mind 2 Cor. v. 10.
[6] Cf. Rom. xiv. 12. [7] Cf. Heb. xii. 28.
[8] On the direct instruction of Polycarp by St. John and his being established by apostolic authority in Smyrna, see Introduction, p. 11.

for what is good,[1] abstaining from things which make to offend, and from false brethren and from them that bear the name of the Lord in hypocrisy,[2] who make vain men to err.

VII. "**For every one that confesseth not that Jesus Christ is come in the flesh is anti-Christ**"[3] (1 John iv. 3). And whosoever confesseth not the witness of the Cross is of the devil,[4] and whosoever perverts the oracles of the Lord[5] to

[1] Cf. 1 Pet. iii. 13, R. V., and Tit. ii. 14.

[2] Cf. 1 Tim. iv. 2; and Hermas, *Sim.* ix. 13, 2.

[3] The verbal difference is so slight that this might be taken as a direct quotation; at the same time it will be remembered that Polycarp was steeped in the verbal teaching of St. John, and this was no doubt an oft repeated saying. Belief in the incarnation is the "articulus" not only "stantis vel cadentis ecclesiæ," but of the state of the individual, and this whether its denial appear in the docetism of the sub-apostolic age, or in the humanitarianism of the nineteenth century.

[4] The witness of the Cross is probably the witness or testimony borne by the Cross, *i. e.* the evidence furnished by the incidents of the Passion. "Perhaps it refers especially to the piercing of the side, and the issue of the blood and water (John xix. 34) as a proof of the reality of Christ's crucified body" (Lightfoot). Cf. also 1 John iii. 8.

[5] The word translated *oracles*, i.e. *logia*, occurs four times in Scripture. In Acts vii. 38 St. Stephen speaks of Moses receiving "lively oracles," the living words of the Decalogue. In Rom. iii. 2 the Jews are said to have been entrusted with the oracles or words of God. In Heb. v. 12 they "have need that one teach them again

his own lusts, and says that there is neither
resurrection nor judgment, this man is the first
begotten of Satan.[1] Wherefore let us leave the
vanity[2] of the many, and their false teaching,
and let us turn to the word delivered to us from

---

the first principles of the oracles of God," and St.
Peter in 1 Pet. iv. 11, writes—" If any speak let it be as
the oracles of God." None of these instances bear out
the restricted meaning which has been attached to the
word by those who understand the work of Papias mentioned by Eusebius (*Ecc. Hist.* iii. 39) to be an exegesis
not of the Gospels but of bare sayings of our Lord, and
has become popularised by the publication in 1897 of the
fragments of sayings of Jesus discovered at Oxyrhynchus
under the title "Logia." Bishop Lightfoot remarks that
" it was natural that Polycarp, who had conversed with
Apostles and personal disciples of Christ, should, like
Papias, refer to our Lord's discourses as Logia, which
might include oral traditions." But there is no strong
reason for supposing that Logia is not used by Polycarp
in the wider and more general sense of Gospel teaching.
On the usage and meaning of the word cf. my note on
Theodoret, *Ecc. Hist.*, p. 155, and Dr. Salmon's Introduction to the study of the New Testament, p. 95, *et seq.*

[1] The expression said by Irenæus to be used by
Polycarp of Marcion (Irenæus, *Hær.* iii. 3, and Euseb.
Hist. Ecc. iii. 39). Cf. pp. 9, 10.

[2] The word occurs in Rom. viii. 20, Eph. iv. 17, and 2
Pet. ii. 18, and is the Greek of the LXX. for the familiar
"Vanity of vanities" of Ecc., and has been popularised
in Thackeray's "*mataiotes mataioteton*" in the poem
'Vanitas Vanitatum.'

the beginning,[1] "**watching unto prayer**"[2] (1 Pet. iv. 7), continuing in fastings, in supplications asking the all-seeing God[3] not to "**lead us into temptation**" (Matt. vi. 13 ; Luke xi. 4), as the Lord said, "**The Spirit indeed is willing, but the flesh is weak**"[4] (Matt. xxvi. 41 and Mark xiv. 38).

VIII. Unfailingly then let us continue in our hope, and in the pledge[5] of our righteousness, which is Christ Jesus, "**Who bare our sins in His**

[1] *i.e.* the "faith once delivered to the Saints" of Jude 3 (cf. chap. i. p. 29). Already the Church is confronted with the two notions of development which have been from time to time among her main difficulties ; (i) the suggestion from without that the Catholic Faith is only the development of a legend, (ii) the suggestion from within that grotesque accretions are the natural development of healthy growth.

[2] Though the present participle is substituted for the i. Aor. Imperative, and we have a slight variation in the phrase, this may be reckoned as a quotation. The verb in the original means to "be sober," and the word rendered in A. V. "Be ye sober," to be temperate ; R. V. "Be ye therefore of sound mind, and be sober unto prayer."

[3] Cf. Clem. *Cor.* §§ lv. and lxiv.

[4] Observe the connection in the mind of the writer between the clause of the Lord's Prayer, and the end urged for prayer in Matt. xxvi. 41. Cf. Hermas, *Vis.* iii. 10.

[5] Cf. 2 Cor. i. 22 and v. 5, and Eph. i. 14. The original word *arrabon* represents the Hebrew of Gen. xxxviii. 17, 18, and passed into Latin as *arrabo* and *arra*, meaning a sum paid down as earnest of the completion of a bargain.

own[1] body on the tree" (1 Pet. ii. 24), "**Who did no sin, neither was guile found in His mouth**" (1 Pet. ii. 22), but on our account, that we may live in Him who endured all things. Let us then become imitators of His patience, and if we be suffering on account of His name, let us glorify Him.[2] For this example[3] He appointed for us through Himself,[4] and this was the profession of our faith.

IX. I therefore call on you all to obey the "**word of righteousness**" (Heb. v. 13) and to practise all patience. This patience you saw face to face not only in the blessed Ignatius and Zosimus and Rufus,[5] but also in others of your own

---

It survives in the French "*arrhes*" and the Scotch "*arles*." Christ's victory over sin and death are as it were the pledge and earnest of the victory of redeemed humanity.

[1] An infinitesimally small variation here.

[2] Hermas, *Sim.* ix. 28, 5, "And you who suffer for His name's sake ought to glorify God;" and *Sim.* vi. 3, 6, "They glorify God in that they were delivered unto me and suffer no longer anything of the evil." Cf. 1 Pet. iv. 16.

[3] The word in 1 Pet. ii. 21, used only there in the New Testament. Cf. Clem. *ad Cor.* v. *ad finem*.

[4] "In His own person," Lightfoot, *i.e.* by means of what He was and did.

[5] Cf. Cap. 1. Probably the chained prisoners mentioned there as escorted by the Philippians on the way to Rome. It has been conjectured that Zosimus and Rufus may have been among the Bithynian Christians sent by

folk,[1] and in Paul himself and the rest of the Apostles.

I call upon you as men persuaded that these did not "**run in vain**" (Phil. ii. 16) but in faith and righteousness, and that they are in the place due to them[2] by the side of the Lord, Whose sufferings they shared.[3] For they did not "**love this present world**" (2 Tim. iv. 10), but Him Who on our behalf died, and on our account by[4] God[5] was raised.

X. In these things then stand, following the example of the Lord, "**steadfast**" (1 Cor. xv. 58) in the faith and "**unmovable**," "**kindly affectioned one to another with brotherly love**"[6] (Rom. xii. 10),

---

Pliny to Rome. Pliny, *Ep.* 97, Zahn, *Ignatius of Antioch*, p. 292, Lightfoot *in loc.* "The Rufus of Polycarp is possibly the same who is mentioned in Rom. xvi. 13, and this latter again may, with some degree of probability, be identified with the son of Simon of Cyrene (Mark xv. 21); but the name is not rare" (Lightfoot).

[1] On early persecutions at Philippi cf. Phil. i. 7, 28, 29, 30.

[2] Cf. Clem. *ad Cor.* v., and for "with the Lord" Phil. i. 23.

[3] Cf. Rom. viii. 17.

[4] Here the Greek MSS. fail, and the text is supplied from Lat. translations and from quotations in Eusebius.

[5] Cf. Ignat. *Rom.* vi.

[6] Of course a conjecture, though almost certain conjecture, of quotation : the Lat. is "fraternitatis amatores diligentes invicem."

partners in the truth, forestalling one another in the gentleness of the Lord, despising no one. While you are able to do good [1] put it not off, because "**Almsgiving delivereth from death**" (Tobit iv. 10 ; xii. 9). "**All of you be subject one to another**" (1 Pet. v. 5), "**having your conversation**" blameless "**among the Gentiles, in order that from your good works**" (1 Pet. ii. 12) both you may receive praise, and your Lord may not be blasphemed in you. But woe unto him by whom the name of the Lord is blasphemed. Teach therefore all men temperance, in which you yourselves have your conversation.

XI. I have been much distressed for Valens,[2] who was once upon a time made a Presbyter among you, that he should be so ignorant of the place [3] assigned him. I exhort you therefore that ye abstain from covetousness, and that ye be chaste and true. "**Abstain from every evil**" (1 Thess. v. 22). How can he who is not able

---

[1] Cf. Prov. iii. 28.

[2] "The name Valens seems to have been common at Philippi. It is found not less than four times on the tablets of one Latin inscription at this place. Corp. *Insc. Lat*. iii. 633" (Lightfoot).

[3] Locus, equivalent to the Greek *topos*, according to Lightfoot having the sense of office. Cf. Acts i. 25, where the better reading is "*place* of ministry." Wake renders "the place given him *in the Church*."

to rule himself in these things preach this
to another? If any man have not abstained
from covetousness he shall be defiled by idolatry
and judged among the Gentiles, who have not
known the judgment of the Lord,[1] or do we not
know that "**the saints shall judge the world**"
(1 Cor. vi. 2), as Paul teacheth? Not that I
have perceived or heard of anything of this kind
in you among whom the blessed Paul laboured
and who were in the beginning [2] his "**epistles**"
(2 Cor. iii. 2). Concerning you he boasts in all
the Churches [3] which alone in those days had
known the Lord: for we had not yet known
Him.[4] Deeply, brethren, am I grieved for him

[1] Cf. Jer. v. 4.

[2] The Latin is "qui *estis* in principio epistulæ ejus."
But this is almost certainly an error in translating the
vague participial form of the Greek. Cf. Lightfoot *in loc.*
For "the beginning" in the sense of the earliest days of
the Gospel cf. i. and note. Cf. also Phil. iv. 15.

[3] Cf. 2 Thess. i. 4.

[4] *i.e.* Smyrna contained no Christians in A.D. 52, when
the Church of Philippi was founded, or in A.D. 53, when
the second Thessalonian Letter was written. "A few
years later, however (Rev. ii. 8), there was an important
Church there. Probably the conversion of Smyrna, as of
Colossæ, was an indirect consequence of St. Paul's long
sojourn at Ephesus. Cf. Acts xix. 10, 26" (Lightfoot). If
we take A.D. 155 as the date of Polycarp's martyrdom, his
own reckoning (*Pol. Mart.* ix.) will give 69 as a date by
which there was a Church in Smyrna.

and for his wife. The Lord grant them genuine repentance.[1] Be ye too, therefore, moderate in this matter, and "**count not**" folk of this sort as "**enemies**" (2 Thess. iii. 15), but call them back as weak[2] and wandering members, that you may keep whole the body of you all,[3] for thus doing ye edify yourselves.

XII. For I am assured that you are well trained in the Holy Scriptures, and that nothing has escaped your attention. This has not been granted to me.[4] Only, as is said in these Scriptures, "**Be ye angry and sin not**" (Ps. iv. 4, LXX), and "**Let not the sun go down on your wrath**"[5] (Eph. iv. 26).

Happy is he who remembers, as I believe you do. But God and the Father of our Lord Jesus Christ and the Eternal High Priest[6] Himself,

---

[1] Cf. 2 Tim. ii. 25.

[2] Lat. passibilia = Grk. *pathela*, applied in a different sense to Christ in Acts xxvi. 23.

[3] Cf. 1 Cor. xii. 26.

[4] Polycarp has a modest estimate of his own knowledge of the Scriptures. Yet his short letter shows considerable acquaintance with them.

[5] Here both Old and New Testaments together are apparently quoted as Scripture, though it may be contended that the term applies only to the verse cited by St. Paul from the Psalms.

[6] Cf. *Pol. Mart.* xiv. and the note there.

Jesus Christ the Son of God,[1] edify you in faith and truth and in all gentleness and meekness; in forbearance, in long-suffering, in patience, in purity; may He grant you part and lot among His Saints, and to us with you, and to all under heaven which are ordained to believe in our Lord and God Jesus Christ, and in His Father "**who raised Him from the dead**" (Gal. i. 1; Col. ii. 12). "**Pray for all Saints**" (Eph. vi. 18). Pray also for kings and for powers and rulers,[2] and "**for them that persecute**" and hate "**you**" (Matt. v. 44), and for the "**enemies of the Cross**" (Phil. iii. 18), that your fruit may be manifest in all,[3] that ye may be perfect in Him.

XIII. Both you and Ignatius have written to me that, if any one go to Syria,[4] he is to con-

---

[1] So the Latin *Dei filius*. Lightfoot, however, gives in his Greek version the Greek equivalent not of "Son of God," but of "God," following quotations in Timotheus Ælurus and Severus of Antioch, and the analogy of the reading "God was manifest in the flesh" in 1 Tim. iii. 16 and "the only begotten God" in John i. 18.

[2] 1 Tim. ii. 1.

[3] Cf. John xv. 16 and 1 Tim. iv. 15.

[4] "There is no direct charge in the letter of Ignatius to Polycarp that the Smyrnæan messenger should carry the letter of the Philippians to Syria. If, therefore, Polycarp has used a rigidly accurate expression here, it will be necessary to suppose that Ignatius had written other

vey the letter also from you. I shall carry out your wish, if I find a favourable opportunity; whether I go myself, or find some one to act the envoy also for you. The letters [1] of Ignatius sent to us by him, and all the rest which we had by us, we have sent to you, as you enjoined. They are attached to this letter. From them you will be able to be greatly benefited, for they embrace faith, patience, and every kind of edification which regards our Lord. If ye have any more certain knowledge concerning Ignatius himself, and those with him, inform us.

XIV. This letter I have written you by Crescens,[2] whom I but now commended to you,

---

instructions (no longer extant) to Polycarp—probably a few lines by way of postscript to the letter of the Philippians. We may observe, however, (1) that Polycarp does not separate the instructions of the Philippians from those of Ignatius, but masses them together; and (2) that Ignatius, writing to Polycarp, does charge him generally to place in the hands of the Smyrnæan delegate the letters of divers Churches which were not able to send messengers of their own. Polycarp, therefore, writing loosely, might very naturally infuse the instructions of Ignatius into the request of the Philippians, as applying indirectly to them, though not immediately referring to them " (Lightfoot).

[1] On the use of the plural for a single letter cf. note on chap. iii. p. 32.

[2] *Crescens* may have been amanuensis, carrier, or both. For the name cf. 2 Tim. iv. 10.

and am still commending ; for his conversation with us was blameless, and so I believe [1] was his conversation with you. His sister you shall have commended to you when she comes to you.

Fare ye well in the Lord Jesus Christ, in grace, with all yours. Amen.

[1] Cf. 2 Tim. i. 5.

VIII

THE LETTER OF THE SMYRNÆANS ON THE MARTYRDOM OF POLYCARP

THE Church of God sojourning at Smyrna to the Church of God sojourning [1] at Philomelium,[2] and to all the dioceses [3] of the Holy Catholic Church [4] in every place, mercy and peace and love of God the Father and of our Lord Jesus Christ be multiplied.[5]

[1] Cf. the Salutation of the Letter of Polycarp.

[2] Identified by Hamilton with the modern *Akshehr*, a place in the plain to the north of the range north of the Pisidian Antioch. Cf. Ramsay, *Hist. Geog. A. M.* p. 140. A Bishop of Philomelium appears at the Council of Constantinople in 381, but between this and the date of the Letter there is no mention of it in Christian literature.

[3] Orig. "parishes." This Lightfoot translates "brotherhoods" and Wake "assemblies." Neither gives the force of the word, which means "place or condition of sojourning": wherever a Christian Church "sojourned", there was a *parœcia* or diocese. Cf. note on Letter of Polycarp, p. 28.

[4] Cf. Ignat. *ad Smyrn.* viii., which is the earliest dated document in which the phrase Catholic Church appears. Cf. p. 20.

[5] Cf. note on Salutation of the Letter of Polycarp.

D

I. We write to you, brethren, the events which befell them that suffered martyrdom, and the blessed Polycarp, who, as it were, by his martyrdom set his seal upon the persecution,[1] and put an end to it. For nearly all the preceding events came to pass in order that to us the Lord might once again give an example of the martyrdom which resembles the Gospel story.[2]

For he waited that he might be betrayed, just as was the Lord, to the end that we too may become imitators of Him, regarding not only what concerns ourselves but also what concerns our neighbours.[3]

For it is the part of true and constant love that a man should wish not only himself, but also all the brethren, to be saved.

II. Now blessed and noble[4] were all the martyrdoms which took place in accordance with the will of God; for we are bound to be very reverent and to ascribe the power over all things to God. And who could fail to marvel

---

[1] *i. e.* the persecution at Smyrna involving the death of Germanicus, Quintus, nine nameless victims, and Polycarp.

[2] *i. e.* nearly all the circumstances of Polycarp's apprehension corresponded with those of the Lord's Passion.

[3] Cf. Phil. ii. 4.

[4] Cf. Clem. *ad Cor.* v.; Mart. *Ig.* ii. and vii.

at their nobility, their endurance, their love for
their Master? Some were so torn by the
scourges [1] that the structure of their flesh to the
inner veins and arteries was exposed to view;
but they endured it, so that even the bystanders
were moved to pity and lamentation. Some
reached such a pitch of noble endurance that
not one of them let cry or groan escape him,
while they showed to us all that tortured as they
were at that time Christ's martyrs were absent
from the flesh [2]; or rather that standing by their
side their Lord was in close converse with them.
So, giving heed to the grace of Christ, they were
despising the torments of the world, redeeming
themselves at the cost of one short season from
everlasting punishment. Cold to them was the
fire of the inhuman tormentors; for they kept
before their eyes their escape from the fire that
is everlasting and is never quenched, while with
the eyes of the heart they looked up at the good
things reserved for them that have endured,
which "**neither ear hath heard nor eye seen, neither**

[1] On the "horribile flagellum" of Roman torture cf.
Horace, *Sat.* I. iii. 119. The scourge was occasionally
fatal in its application. The verb translated "torn"
means literally "thoroughly carded." For its use of in-
jurious violence to the human body cf. Eurip. *Supp.*
503.

[2] Cf. 2 Cor. v. 6.

have entered into the hearts of man" (1 Cor. ii. 9, slightly varied), but were being shown by the Lord to those who were now already no longer men but angels.　In like manner they that were condemned to the beasts underwent awful punishments, being made to lie on prickly shells [1] and buffeted,[2] with various other forms of torture, to the end that, if it were possible, by means of their protracted punishment they might be turned to denial by him who was devising so many wiles against them—the devil.

III. But thanks be to God, for He verily prevailed against all.[3]　For the right noble

---

[1] Lit. "heralds," or "trumpeters," κῆρυξ being the Greek name for a mollusc, Lat. the "*buccinum*," which was used as a means of torture. Eusebius in his narrative of the martyrdom adds the explanation "heralds *out of the sea*." "Sea-shells, potsherds and the like, appear not unfrequently as instruments of torture in the accounts of martyrdoms : *Act. S. Vincent.* 7 ; *Act. Tarach. Prob. etc.* 3 ; *B. Felicis Conf. Vit.* in Bedæ, Op. v. 790, ed. Migne" (Lightfoot).

[2] Cf. 1 Pet. ii. 20, as well as 1 Cor. iv. 11, and 2 Cor. xii. 7.

[3] So Lightfoot, in accordance with the Latin "Gratia domino nostro Jesu Christo qui contra omnes fidus servorum suorum defensor adsistit," and correcting the Greek οὐκ,' not,' into οὖν, 'verily.' An alternative reading would be to make *the devil* the subject of prevail, and to render for he did not prevail against all ; *i. e.* he only prevailed against one, Quintus turned renegade.

Germanicus [1] by means of his endurance, turned their cowardice into courage. With signal distinction did he fight against the beasts. While the Proconsul,[2] wishful to persuade him, was urging him to have compassion on his youth, in his eagerness to be released the sooner from their unrighteous and careless mode of life he used force to the wild beast and pulled it on himself. Now it was on this that all the multitude, amazed at the noble conduct of the Godbeloved and Godfearing race of the Christians, shouted out, "Away with the Atheists. Let search be made for Polycarp."

IV. But one of them, Quintus by name, a Phrygian,[3] lately arrived from his native

---

[1] He is traditionally "the boy" Germanicus, cf. Eusebius (*Hist. Ecc.* iv. 155), and Lightfoot, "the brave youth." I do not know of any authority for this except the phrase of Eusebius ; for the word ἡλικία, the term in the text of the original for that which Germanicus should pity, rendered by Lightfoot *youth*, might as well mean *old age*, and is so used of Polycarp himself in chap. vii. The Latin represents it by *ætas*, which is equally indeterminate, but more likely to stand for age than for youth.

[2] For the official title of Acts xiii. 7, 8, 12 ; xix. 38, cf. chap. xxi., where the name is given as *Statius Quadratus*.

[3] The Phrygians were proverbially cowards. So Tertullian, *de Anim.* xx. "Comici Phrygas timidos illudunt," and the proverb "more cowardly than a Phrygian hare." Strab. l. ii. 30.

province, when he saw the beasts, was afraid.
It was he who had forced both himself and certain others to come forward of their own accord.
After very earnest entreaty he had been persuaded by the Proconsul to take the oath and
offer incense. Now, brethren, we do not com-
mend those who surrender themselves, for not
such is the teaching of the Gospel.[1]

V. Now the most admirable Polycarp so soon
as he heard [that he was being sought for] at
first showed no dismay, but wished to remain in
town. The majority, however, prevailed on him
to withdraw. And withdraw he did, to a little
estate[2] not far from the city. There he spent
his time with a few companions, occupied night
and day in nothing but prayer for all men, and
for the Churches throughout the world,[3] as indeed

---

[1] Cf. Matt. x. 23; John vii. 30; viii. 59; x. 39. Lightfoot
quotes Zahn, "A communi priscæ ecclesiæ sententia Ter-
tullianus recessit cum fugiendum in persecutione non esse
studeret demonstrare." Tertullian's view was that our
Lord made only a special concession for special times
(*de Fuga*, 4). On the general opinion of the early Church
cf. Greg. Naz. *Orat.* i.; and Athanasius, *Apol. de Fuga*.

[2] Probably his own property. The natural inference
from the narrative is that the property and slaves were
his own. "This supposition at all events agrees with
the old story that he possessed considerable property"
(Lightfoot).

[3] Cf. Pol. *ad Philip*. vi.

was his constant habit. And while praying he fell into a trance three days before his apprehension, and he saw his pillows being burned by fire. And he turned and said to them that were with him, "I must needs be burned alive."

VI. Now his pursuers were persistent, so he shifted his quarters to another farm. Then straightway the pursuers arrived on the spot and, on failing to find him, they seized two slave-boys. One of these confessed under torture; for indeed it was impossible for him to evade pursuit, since they that betrayed him were of his own household. And the head of the police,[1] who, as it befell, bore the same name [as our Lord's judge], being called Herod, made haste to bring him into the stadium, in order that he might be made a partner of Christ, and so fulfil his own appointed lot, and that his betrayers might undergo the punishment of Judas himself.

VII. Accordingly, having the lad with them, on Friday at about supper-time forth sallied

---

[1] Or " Peace magistrate," εἰρήναρχος. The title appears frequently in inscriptions. *Vide* Lightfoot *in loc.*, who says, " in some respects 'the High-Sheriff' would be a nearer equivalent. Our phrase 'Justice of the Peace' is analogous." Cf. 'Friedensrichter' and 'Juge de Paix.'

constables [1] and mounted men, with their usual equipment, hurrying as though "**against a thief**" (Matt. xxvi. 55). Late in the day they came up together and found him in a cottage lying in an upper room. It was within his power to go away thence to another place, but he refused to do so, saying, "God's will be done." [2] So, on hearing of their arrival, he came down and conversed with them, they all the while wondering at his age and his constancy, and at there being so much ado about the arrest of such an old man. Upon this he gave orders for something to be served for them to eat and drink, at that hour, as much as they would. He besought them withal to give him an hour that he might pray freely; and on their granting him this boon he stood up [3] and prayed, being so full of

---

[1] The word διωγμῖται or διωγμεῖται, literally "pursuers," had passed into a technical term for a kind of police. So in *Amm. Marcell.*, xxvii. 9: "Semiermibus quos diocmitas appellant." They were under the orders of the cirenarch or justice of the peace. Cf. Lightfoot *in loc.*

[2] Cf. Acts xxi. 14; Matt. vi. 10, xxvi. 42; Luke xxii. 42.

[3] The original is a passive participle = "on being set up." Cf. the Pharisee in Luke xviii. 11, where a formal posture seems to be contrasted with the simpler "standing" of the Publican. It is used of our Lord in Luke xviii. 40, and of Zaccheus in Luke xix. 8.

the grace of God, that for the space of two hours he could not hold his peace, while the hearers were smitten with amazement, and many were sorry that they had come after so venerable an old man.

VIII. After remembering all, both small and great, high and low, who had ever been brought into communication with him, and all the Catholic Church throughout the world, at last he brought his prayer to an end. The time had come for him to depart. They set him on an ass[1] and brought him into the city, it being a high Sabbath.[2] He was met by the eirenarch Herodes, and by his father, Nicetes,[3] who shifted him into their carriage,[4] and tried to persuade him as they sate by his side, urging, "Why, what harm is there in saying Cæsar is

---

[1] Possibly a detail recorded because it helped to bear out the idea of the martyrdom "according to the Gospel."

[2] Cf. note on Chap. xxi. p. 72.

[3] "The name occurs more than once in the inscriptions at Smyrna, and in the neighbourhood. *Corp. Inscr. Græc.* 3148, 3359. As it is not a common name until a later date, this fact is not without its value" (Lightfoot).

[4] καροῖχα = Lat. carruca, a conveyance of ceremony, used on State occasions. Cf. Suet. *Nero*, 30, on Nero's luxurious progresses.

Lord,[1] and sacrificing,[2] and the rest of it, and so saving thyself?" At first he made no reply, but, as they were persistent, he said, "I do not intend to do what you advise me." On their failing to persuade him they began to use terrible language and to drag him hurriedly down, so that as he was getting down from the carriage he grazed his shin. Without turning back, as though he had suffered no hurt, he fared on with speed, and was conducted to the stadium, where there was so great a tumult that it was impossible for any one to be heard.

IX. Now as Polycarp was entering into the stadium, there came a voice to him from heaven, "Be strong, Polycarp, and play the man."[3] The

[1] So in the Greek MSS. Eusebius has the vocative "Lord Cæsar," which is followed by Wake, and so the Latin. Of course there was a sense in which Cæsar might be called Lord with propriety, as Tertullian, *Apol.* xxxiv., "Dicam plane imperatorem dominum, sed more communi, sed quando non cogor ut Dominum Dei vice dicam," and Donata in the "Passion of the Scillitan martyrs" (A.D. 180), "Honour to Cæsar as Cæsar, but fear to God." The singular number here and in Chap. ix. is in favour of the martyrdom happening under the sole sovereignty of a single Emperor.

[2] *i.e.* offering incense. This use of the word illustrates the fact that θύω in Greek, like "sacrifice" in English, does not necessarily mean "kill."

[3] Cf. Josh. i. 6, 7, 9. The incident is cited by Lightfoot

speaker indeed no one saw, but the voice was heard by those of our friends who were present. Then he was dragged forward, and great was the din of them that heard that Polycarp was arrested. So he was brought before the Proconsul,[1] who asked him if he were the man himself? He assented, and the Proconsul tried to persuade him, urging, " Have respect to thine old age," and the rest of it, according to the customary form, " Swear by the genius[2] of Cæsar ; repent ; say, ' Away with the Atheists ! ' " Then Polycarp looked with a serious counten-

---

as a further item in the Gospel parallel. But the voice in John xii. 28 was for the assurance of the bystanders, not for the encouragement of the Sufferer. The voice in the text is hardly miraculous. The words were such as might naturally have been used by any brave Christian present, and in the deafening disturbance kept up by the crowd might easily be thought to come "from heaven."

[1] Cf. note on chap. iii. p. 53.

[2] On this common deification of the reigning Cæsar, cf. the Bætic inscription quoted by Lightfoot from *Corp. Inscr. Lat.* ii. 1963, 1964. " Per Jovem et Divom Augustum et Divom Claudium et Divom Vespasianum Augustum et Divom Titum Augustum et *genium Imperatoris Domitiani Augusti* Deosque Penates," also " Sic eorum numen vocant, ad imagines supplicant, genium, id est dæmonem ejus, implorant," Minuc. Felix, xxix.; and Origen, *C. Celsum*, viii. 65 : " We do not swear by the genius of the Emperor."

ance on the multitude of lawless heathen gathered in the stadium, and he beckoned with his hand, and looked up to heaven with a groan and said, "Away with the Atheists." The Proconsul continued insisting and saying, "Swear, and I release thee; revile the Christ." And Polycarp said, "Eighty and six years have ·I served Him, and He hath done me no wrong : how then can I blaspheme my King Who saved me?"[1]

X. The Proconsul continuing to persist, and to urge, "Swear by the genius of Cæsar," he answered, "If thou vainly fanciest that I would 'swear by the genius of Cæsar,' as thou sayest, pretending that thou art ignorant who I am,

---

[1] No certain inference can be drawn from this passage as to the precise age of Polycarp. The Saint must mean to reckon his service from his Baptism, and how near this was to his birth we do not know. St. Jerome in his *Life of Hilarion* (§ xlv.) makes Hilarion, agèd seventy-nine (§ xliv.), exclaim, "Egredere anima mea ; quid dubitas? Septuaginta prope annis servisti Christo, et mortem times?" He was then about ten years old at his baptism. If Polycarp was a slave, and not the child of Christian parents, baptism at about the same age might be probable in his case ; and this is precisely the tradition enshrined in the *Life* by Pionius. The little lad bought by the devout lady Callisto, at the Ephesian Gate of Smyrna, may well have been about ten, and would no doubt have been soon after baptized (Vit. *Pion.* iii.). But this would make him 95 or 96 at his death.

hear plainly that I am a Christian. And if thou art willing to learn the doctrine of Christianity, appoint a day,[1] and grant me a hearing." The Proconsul said, " Persuade the people." [2] Polycarp then said, " Thee, indeed, I should have deemed worthy of argument, for we have been taught to render to authorities and powers ordained by God, honour as is meet,[3] so long as it does us no harm, but I deem not yon multitude worthy of my making my defence to them." [4]

XI. The Proconsul said, " I have wild beasts ; if thou wilt not change thy mind I will throw thee to them." Then he said, " Bid them be brought : change of mind from better to worse is not a change that we are allowed ; but to change from wrong to right is good." Then again said the Proconsul to him, " As thou despisest the

---

[1] Cf. the Latin "diem dicere," to grant a trial, and 1 Cor. iv. 3, where "man's judgment" is literally "man's day."

[2] "It is not clear with what motive the Proconsul says this ; whether (1) like Pilate, with a sincere desire to release the prisoner, or (2) as an excuse for his execution, knowing such an appeal to be useless" (Lightfoot).

[3] Cf. Rom. xiii. 1, and 1 Pet. ii. 13.

[4] On the uselessness of pleading to the mob cf. Matt. vii. 6.

beasts, unless thou change thy mind, I make thee to be destroyed by fire." Then Polycarp: "Thou threatenest the fire that burns for a season, and after a little while is quenched; for thou art ignorant of the fire of the judgment to come, and of everlasting punishment reserved for the ungodly. But for what art thou waiting? Bring what thou wilt."

XII. While speaking these words and many more he was filled with courage and gladness: his face grew full of grace, so that not only did it not fall, agitated at all that was being said to him, but on the contrary the Proconsul was amazed, and sent his own crier to make proclamation in the middle of the stadium thrice, "Polycarp has confessed himself to be a Christian." No sooner was this proclaimed by the crier than the whole multitude, both of Gentiles and of Jews [1] dwelling at Smyrna, with ungovernable rage and a loud voice began to shout—"This is the teacher of Asia, the father of the Christians, the destroyer of our Gods, the man who teaches many not to sacrifice nor even to worship." With these words they kept up their shout and continued asking Philip the Asiarch [2]

---

[1] On Jews at Smyrna cf. Rev. ii. 8, and, on their activity in persecuting Christians, Euseb. *Hist. Ecc.* v. 16.

[2] "The Asiarch was the head of the confederation of

to let loose a lion at Polycarp. "But," said he, "that is no longer in my power : the sports are over."[1] Thereupon it was their pleasure to yell with one accord that he should burn Polycarp alive. For the [prediction] of the vision about his pillow must needs be fulfilled, on the occasion of his seeing it burning while he was at prayer, and turning round and saying prophetically to his faithful friends, " I must needs be burnt alive."

---

the principal cities of the Roman province of Asia. As such he was the chief priest of Asia and president of the games." " Under the Roman government the principal cities of the several provinces were united together in confederations for certain religious and civil purposes called *commune* Bithyniæ, Ciliciæ, Galatiæ, Pamphyliæ, etc. The presiding officers of these unions bore the titles Bithyniarch, Galatarch, etc." "In six at least of the cities comprised in the *commune Asiæ* (Smyrna, Ephesus, Pergamum, Sardes, Philadelphia and Cyzicus) periodical festivals and games were held under the auspices of the confederation" (Lightfoot). The plural in Acts xix. 31 may be explained either (1) by the theory that retired Asiarchs retained the honorary title, or (2) that the title may have been given to the chief priests of the imperial worship in the cities of the confederation. See a full discussion of the whole subject in Lightfoot's Appendix on the Asiarchate, *Apost. Fathers*, II. iii. p. 404.

[1] The word κυνηγέσια, = lit. dog drives, corresponds with the Latin *venationes*, and includes all fights with beasts in the circus, either with or without dogs.

XIII. This then was no sooner said than done, the mob in a moment getting together logs and fagots from the workshops and baths, the Jews as usual showing themselves specially zealous in the work. When the pyre had been made ready, Polycarp took off all his upper garments, and untied his girdle. He endeavoured also to take off his shoes, though he had never been in the habit of doing this, because every one of the faithful was eager to be the first to touch his bare body. For his good life's sake he had been treated with every honour even before his head was white. Forthwith then all the gear adapted for the pyre was put about him. They were on the point of fastening him with nails, but he said, " Let me be as I am : He that gave me power to abide the fire will grant me too without your making me fast with nails to abide untroubled [1] at the pyre."

XIV. So they did not nail him, but they bound him to [the stake]. He put his hands behind him and was bound, like a goodly ram out of a great flock for an offering, a whole burnt

---

[1] The word of the Moscow MS., ἄσκυλτος, means literally unflayed or unmangled. The cognate verb σκύλλω = flay, had come to mean bore, vex, trouble : so in St. Mark v. 35 it is the word for " why *troublest* thou the Master ? "

offering made ready and acceptable to God. Then he looked up to heaven and said, "O Lord God Almighty, Father of Thy beloved and blessed Son Jesus Christ, by Whose means we have received our knowledge of Thee, God of Angels and Powers and of all creation and of the whole race of the just who live before Thy face, I bless Thee in that Thou hast deemed me worthy of this day and hour; that I might take a portion in the number of the martyrs in the cup of Christ, to the resurrection of eternal life [1] both of soul and body in the incorruption of the Holy Ghost. Among these may I to-day be welcome [2] before Thy face as a fat and acceptable sacrifice as Thou didst prepare and manifest beforehand and didst bring about its fulfilment, Thou the faithful and true God. For this cause, yet and for all things I praise Thee, I bless Thee,[3] I glorify Thee through the everlasting

---

[1] Cf. John v. 29.

[2] The word in the original denotes more than mere reception or acceptance. In Demosthenes 1317, 6, and Plat. *Legg.* 708. A., it=to receive into citizenship. It almost always implies to receive favourably. It is St. Luke's word (xv. 2) for receiveth sinners, and St. Paul's (Romans xvi. 2) for the welcome asked for Phœbe and for Epaphroditus (Phil. ii. 29).

[3] Cf. the Gloria in Excelsis.

and heavenly High Priest[1] Jesus Christ Thy beloved Son, through Whom to Thee with Him and with the Holy Ghost be glory now and for the ages to come. Amen."[2]

XV. When he had offered up his Amen and completed his prayer the firemen kindled the fire. A great flame flashed out, and we to whom it was granted to see saw a marvel; and we moreover were preserved to the end that we might tell to the rest the tidings of what came to pass. The fire made the appearance of a vaulted roof,[3] like a ship's sail filling out with the wind, and it walled about the body of the martyr in a ring. There was it in the midst, not like flesh burning, but like a loaf baking, or like gold and silver being fired in a furnace.

[1] Cf. Pol. *ad Phil.* xii. and Heb. *passim* for the presentation of our Lord as the great High Priest. In Clem. *ad Cor.* He is the High Priest of our oblations.

[2] On the form of the Doxology, cf. St. Basil, *de Sp. Scto.* xxvii.

[3] Cf. the account of the death of Savonarola (*Villari*, ii. 302). "A blast of wind diverted the fire for some time from the three bodies;" and of Bishop Hooper (Foxe, *Acts and Monuments*): "The wind having full strength in that place (it was a cold and lowering morning) it blew the flame from him, so that he was in a manner no more but touched by the fire." So of St. Agnes it was related that when on the pyre she was unharmed by the divided flames. (*Act. Sanct. Boll.* ii. 716.)

Moreover we were aware of a fragrance as great as of frankincense or some other of the precious spices breathing forth [its perfume].[1]

XVI. In the end, when the wicked ones had seen that his body could not be consumed by the fire they commanded an executioner to come up to him and to drive in a dagger. When he had so done there came out [a dove[2] and] abund-

[1] "This phenomenon, however we may explain it, whether from the fragrance of the wood or in some other way, meets us constantly." Cf. A. Harnack in *Zeitschr. f. Kirchengesch.* ii. p. 291. Lightfoot, *Ap. Fathers*, II. i. p. 615.

[2] "These words 'dove and' are wanting not only in all the extant Greek MSS., and in the Latin of Rufinus and in the Syriac Version, but also in writers like Nicephorus, a borrower from Eusebius, who omits them" (Lightfoot). Probably the words were added by the author of the spurious Pionian biography, or by some other late editor. The idea of a dove personifying the ascending soul of the sufferer was familiar to the legendary martyrologist, and finds one of its most famous expressions in the lines of Prudentius († c. 410) on the martyrdom of St. Eulalia—

> "Flamma crepans volat in faciem,
> Perque comas vegetata caput
> Occupat, exsuperatque apicem :
> Virgo, cito cupiens obitum,
> Appetit et bibit ore rogum.
> Emicat inde columba repens,
> Martyris os nive candidior
> Visa relinquere, et astra sequi :

ance of blood so that it put out the fire, and all the multitude marvelled at the mighty difference between the unbelievers and the elect, of whom one was this man, the most admirable Polycarp, who in our times was an apostolic and prophetic teacher, bishop of the Holy[1] Church in Smyrna ; for every word which he uttered from his mouth was accomplished and will be accomplished.

Spiritus hic erat Eulaliæ
Lacteolus, celer, innocuus."

Peristeph. iii. 106.

It may be that the words περιστερὰ καὶ, *i. e.* "a dove and" got into the text by a not unnatural corruption. If the Smyrnæan scribe wrote ΕΞΗΛΘΕΝΠΕΡΙϹΤΕΡΝΑΠΛΗΘΟϹ, *i. e.* "There came out about the breast abundance," it is obvious that this might easily have become ΕΞΗΛΘΕΝΠΕΡΙϹΤΕΡΑΚΑΙΠΛΗΘΟϹ, *i. e.* "There came out a dove and abundance." The most ingenious suggestion, adopted by Zahn, Funk, and Lagarde, is that of Bishop Ch. Wordsworth (App. C. to his *Hippolytus*, pp. 318, 319) that the original was ΕΞΗΛΘΕΝΠΕΡΙϹΤΥΡΑΚΑΠΛΗΘΟϹ, *i. e.* "There came out about the haft abundance." The objection is that στύραξ, the Greek for the spike at the butt-end of a spear (Xen. *Hell.* vi. 2-19), is not known to mean the haft or hilt of a sword or dagger. Bishop Lightfoot inclines to the belief that the words "dove and" were "deliberately added by the spurious Pionius" (*Ap. Fathers*, II. i. pp. 606-643).

[1] The common reading is *Catholic* Church. Bishop Lightfoot is of opinion that the MS. authority is strongly in favour of *Holy.* Cf. *Int.* p. 20.

XVII. But when the jealous, envious evil one, the adversary of the race of the righteous, saw both the majesty of his martyrdom and his blameless conversation from the beginning, and that he was crowned with the crown of incorruption and had carried off a prize which could not be gainsaid, he contrived that not even his poor body should be taken up by us, though many were desirous so to do and to come into communion with his most holy flesh.[1] So he prompted Nicetes, father of Herodes and brother of Alce,[2] to entreat the magistrate not to grant his body, lest, as he said, we should forsake the Crucified, and begin to worship this man. This was done at the prompting and persistence of

[1] *i. e.* "by gathering together about his grave for the purpose of common worship" (Lightfoot). This may be the germ of the sentiment which finds a more distinct expression in St. Basil's Homily on the Forty Martyrs of Sebaste (*Hom.* xix.): "The afflicted flees to the Forty; the joyous hurries to them; the former that he may find relief from his troubles, the latter that his blessings may be preserved . . . Let your supplications be made with the martyrs." The idea is not as the Jesuit annotator Garnier writes, "invocantur martyres ;" it is the fellowship rather than the intercession of the saints which is sought, and this a fellowship localised at their graves. Cf. my note on St. Basil in Nicene and Post-nicene Fathers (*Proleg.* p. lxxi.).

[2] Cf. Ig. *Smyr.* xiii., *Pol.* viii., and p. 23. She was presumably a Christian.

the Jews. They moreover watched, when we were about to try to take him out of the fire, ignorant that it will never at any time be possible for us to abandon the Christ,—Who, blameless on behalf of sinners, suffered for the salvation of the whole world of them that are being saved,—and to worship some other. Him, in that He is Son of God, we adore [1]; the martyrs, as disciples and imitators of the Lord we reverence [2] as they deserve on account of their unsurpassable good will to their own King and Teacher. With them may it be granted to us to be made sharers alike of lot and of learning!

XVIII. When the centurion saw the opposition raised by the Jews, he put him in the midst, and, as their custom is, burned him. So we afterwards took up his bones, more valuable than precious stones, and finer than fine gold, and laid them where it was fitting.[3] There the Lord will permit us, as shall be possible to us, to assemble ourselves together in joy and gladness, and to celebrate the birthday of his martyrdom,

---

[1] προσκυνοῦμεν.   [2] ἀγαπῶμεν.

[3] The place is not revealed for prudence' sake. The Letter of Polycrates, Bp. of Ephesus, writing about A.D. 190, quoted in Euseb. *Hist. Eccl.* v. 24, indicates that he knew of the grave at Smyrna. (κεκοίμηται = hath been laid in his κοιμητήριον, cemetery, or sleeping-place. Cf. Jer *de Vir. Illust.* xlv. "cubat.")

alike in memory of them that have fought before, and for the training and preparation of them that are to fight hereafter.[1]

XIX. Thus it befell the blessed Polycarp, who was martyred with them that came from Philadelphia, himself and eleven others, in Smyrna, and is himself alone held in all men's memory, so that even among the heathen is he everywhere spoken of, as one who was not merely an illustrious teacher, but also a conspicuous martyr. His martyrdom all men are eager to copy, in that it came to pass according to the gospel of Christ. Through his patience he overcame the unrighteous ruler, and thus received [2] the crown of incorruption. Rejoicing with Apostles and all just men, he glorifies our Almighty God and Father, and blesses our Lord Jesus Christ, Saviour of our souls, and Helmsman of our bodies, and Shepherd of the Catholic Church throughout the world.

XX. You did indeed request that the circumstances might be narrated to you more fully. We have, however, for the present, sent you concise information through our brother Marcian. On becoming acquainted with these events, send

[1] Cf. Tert. *de Cor.* iii. "We make offerings for the dead on a yearly day for a birthday."

[2] The word is the same as that in Gal. iv. 5, "received as his due." It is so used in Xen. *Anab.* vii. 7, 14.

on our letter to brethren also beyond, that they may glorify the Lord who makes choice of His own servants. Now unto Him that is able by His grace and gift to bring us all into His heavenly kingdom, through His only-begotten Son, Jesus Christ, be glory, honour, might, majesty, for ever. Salute all the saints. They that are with us, and Euarestus, who wrote the letter, with his whole house, salute you.[1]

XXI. The blessed Polycarp was martyred on the second day of the first part of the month Xanthicus, on the seventh day before the Kalends of March,[2] at the eighth hour,[3] on a great Sabbath.[4] He was apprehended by Herodes

[1] "The name Euarestus occurs three times in Smyrnæan inscriptions . . . The only Bishop of Rome bearing this name is said to have been a Palestinian Jew, but the tradition has no value."—Lightfoot *in loc.*

[2] *i. e.* Feb. 23. The second day of the sixth month is confirmed by the Acts of Pionius ; cf. note on p. 13.

[3] Either 8 a.m., counting from midnight ; or 2 p.m. counting from 6 a.m. The former is the more probable.

[4] Cf. chap. viii. "The mention of the 'Great Sabbath' accords with the statement in the document itself ; and, so far as it goes, is an indication of the same authorship." — Lightfoot. *The* great Sabbath in the Church was the Saturday between Good Friday and Easter (cf. Chrysost. *Op.* v. p. 525). *The* great Sabbath in later Jewish nomenclature was the Sabbath preceding the Passover. In the text "a" great Sabbath may be any Saturday connected with a great Jewish anniversary.

in the Chief Priestship[1] of Philip of Tralles, in the proconsulship of Statius Quadratus,[2] but in the reign of the eternal King, Jesus Christ ; to Whom be honour, glory, dominion through the eternal from generation to generation. Amen.

XXII. (1) We bid you God-speed, brethren, while you are walking by the word of Jesus Christ, according to the Gospel, with Whom be glory to God for the salvation of His holy elect ; even as the blessed Polycarp testified.[3] Be it ours to be found in His footsteps in the Kingdom of Jesus Christ.

(2) This was transcribed by Gaius from the (writings) of Irenæus, a disciple of Polycarp, who also lived with Irenæus.

The martyrdom moreover occurred during a heathen festival. Bishop Lightfoot suggests the games of the Asiatic Confederation (κοινὰ 'Ασίας), in his exhaustive discussion of the whole subject, in *Apost. Fathers*, Part ii. vol. i.

[1] Asiarch and High Priest indicate the same office. Caius Julius Philippus of Tralles is mentioned in an Olympian inscription as Asiarch in A.D. 149. The office may have been held for several years, or more than once.

[2] The assignment of the martyrdom to A.D. 155 depends mainly on the correctness of the year of the proconsulship of Quadratus, accepted by Lightfoot, on the authority of Waddington's chronology of Aristides ; *i. e.* A.D. 154, 155. This fixes the Feb. 23 as the Feb. 23 in 155, in which year it fell on a Saturday. But the evidence is not conclusive. Cf. also Dr. Salmon in *D. C. Biography*, iv. p. 430.   [3] Or suffered martyrdom.

(3) I Socrates in Corinth, from the copy of Gaius, have written it. Grace be with all. ·

(4) I again Pionius from the previous copy have written it. I searched it out in consequence of a revelation, for the blessed Polycarp showed it me in a revelation, as I shall declare in the sequel. I gathered it together now it was nearly worn out with age, that I too may be gathered together by the Lord Jesus Christ with His elect into His heavenly kingdom, to Whom be glory with Father and Holy Ghost, for ever and ever. Amen.[1]

---

[1] These supplementary chapters obviously fall into three divisions, probably distinct in age and authorship. (1) The chronological appendix in Chapter xxi. This is accepted by Bishop Lightfoot as part of the original letter, containing as it does historical references, of which the veracity has received remarkable vindication from recent archæological discovery. (2) Commendatory postscript (xxii. 1). This second postscript is omitted in the Moscow manuscript, and in the Latin version. It is however accepted by Bishop Lightfoot as probably genuine, there being nothing in the words themselves suggestive of a later date. "May not this postscript," he suggests, "have been an appendix added by the Philomelian Church when they forwarded copies of the letter, as they were charged to do, to churches more distant from Smyrna than themselves?"—*Apost. Fathers*, Parts ii. iii. p. 638. (3) (xxii. 2, 3, 4.)—This account of transmission and transcription may probably be referred to the spurious Pionius.

INDEX OF SCRIPTURAL

PASSAGES IN THE EPISTLE

GENERAL INDEX